DINNIS

THE FLYING CAR

By Tai Milo

LCCN: 2024921387
ISBN:
9798218528263
Written and Illustrated by Tai Milo
Illustrations: marker & pencil
with additional adobe illustrator digital photoshop
Text print: The Seasons & Bryndan Write
Editor: Rosalie Bardo

Printed in the United States

Can you find the hidden  throughout the book?

Chapter 1

Play DAY!

One day Dinnis
was making a comic,
until his friend
Brin came over.

They drove outside
to play.

Then tossed the ball
back and forth.

Later, they played hide and seek.

1...2...3...4...5...6...
ready or not...

It's Superhero time!

Then Dinnis and Brin drove to their treehouse.

CHAPTER 2

Dinnis and Brin were
searching for their box
of costumes.

But they couldn't find it.

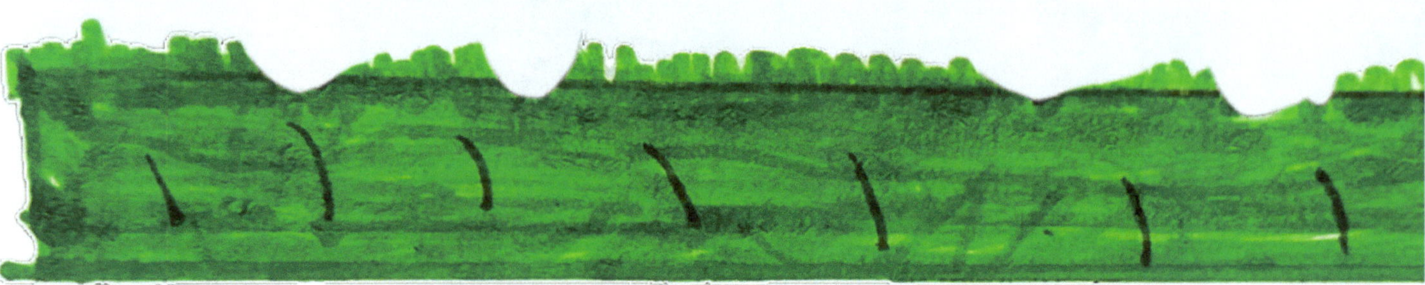

Where is that box?
I know it's here! Keep looking!

"Here it is!", Brin said.
And they began to dress up!

Dinnis had a surprise for Brin.
He put on his cape,
then jumped from the treehouse.

Yaaahoooo!

Dinnis began to fly towards VroomsVille.

So, Brin followed him into the city.

I will help you get down.
Help!
My bumper is
stuck in the tree.

Dinnis helped the little car down
and was ready to zoom back home.

Brin was very proud of his buddy.

Back at home, they celebrated by eating pizza.
This was the best day ever!

Dinnis said goodbye to Brin,
then thanked him for
coming to play.

The  End

Help Dinnis find his way back to Vroomsville.
VroomsVille

Thank you for reading!

Tai is a 9- year- old self-taught pianist, avid Minecraft builder, and eccentric creator.

He enjoys drawing unique characters then making books about them.

See you in the next adventure!
Social Media: @BuildingwithTai